Press out stickers, moisten, and place them on the pages where they belong. Finish the pictures with your crayons.

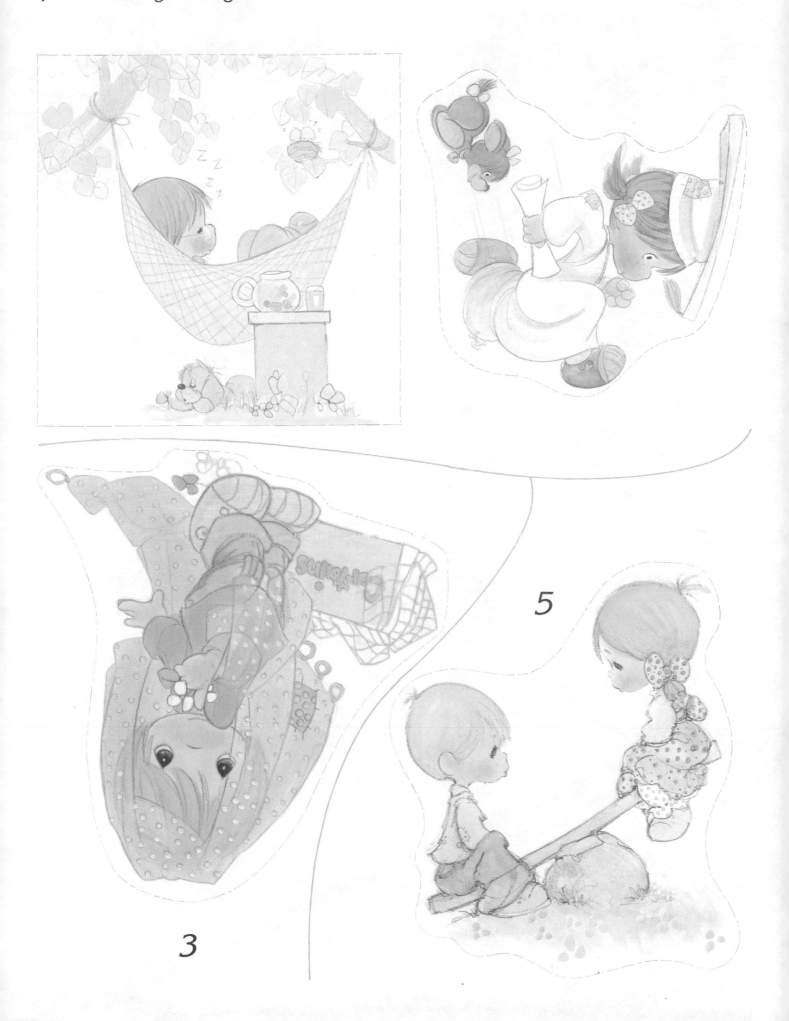

RUN A LAP.

TAKE A NAP.

MAKE A FRIEND.

JUST PRETEND.

BE A CLOWN.

GO UP AND DOWN.

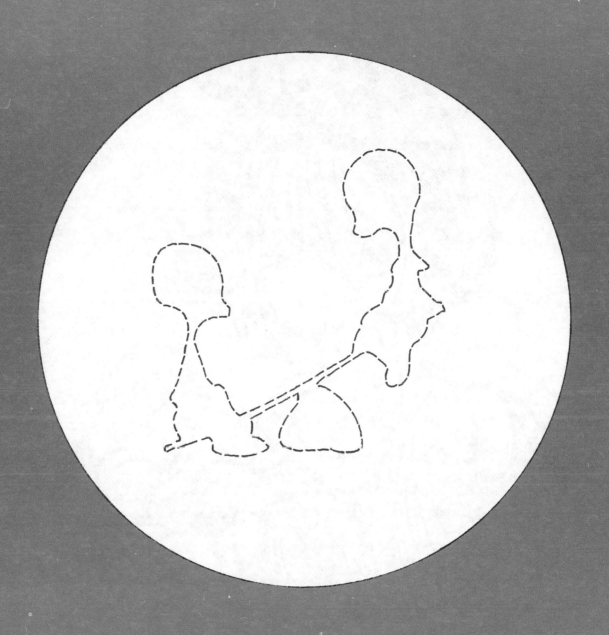

DO A FAVOR.

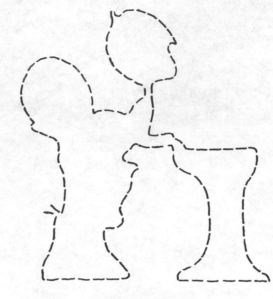

TASTE A FLAVOR.

7

8

15

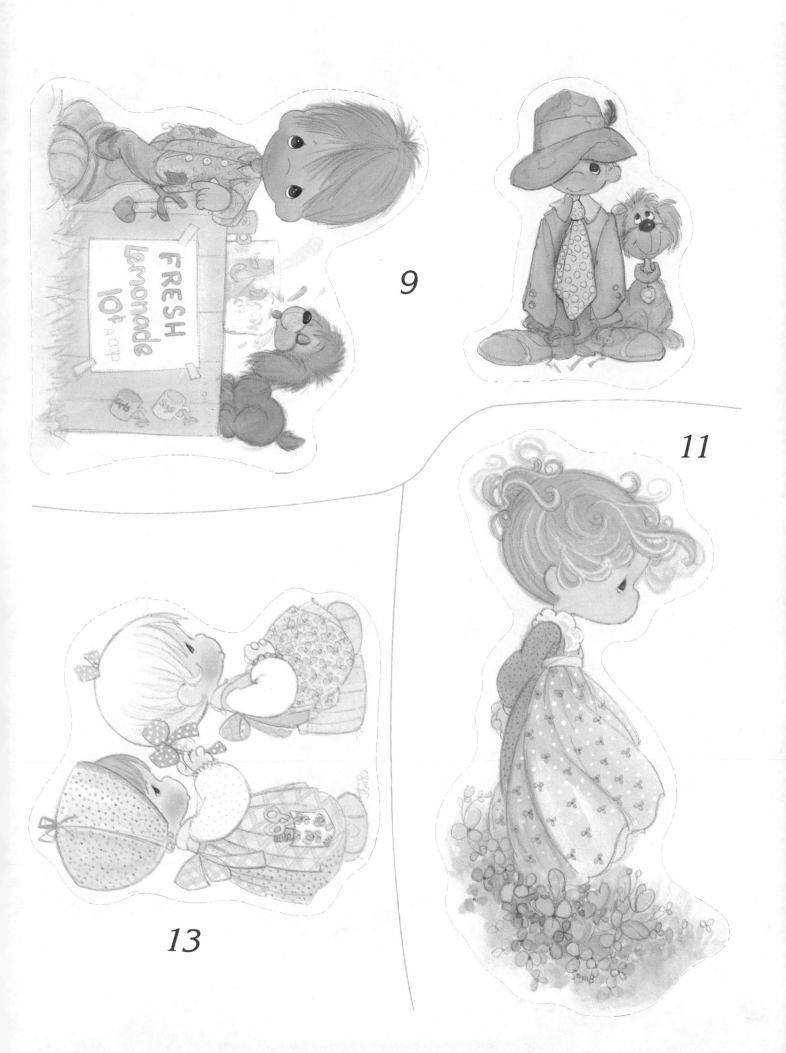

FRESH
Lemonade
10¢ A CUP

9

11

13

WATCH YOUR PUP!

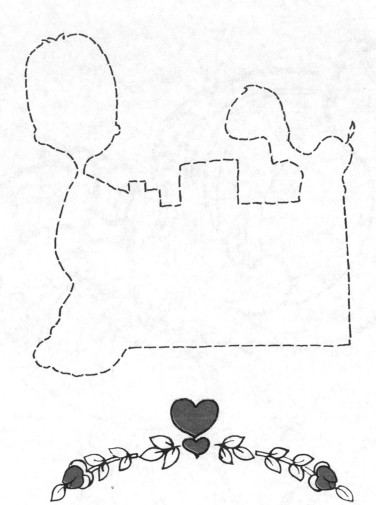

GET ALL DRESSED UP.

SAIL THE SEAS.

FEEL THE BREEZE.

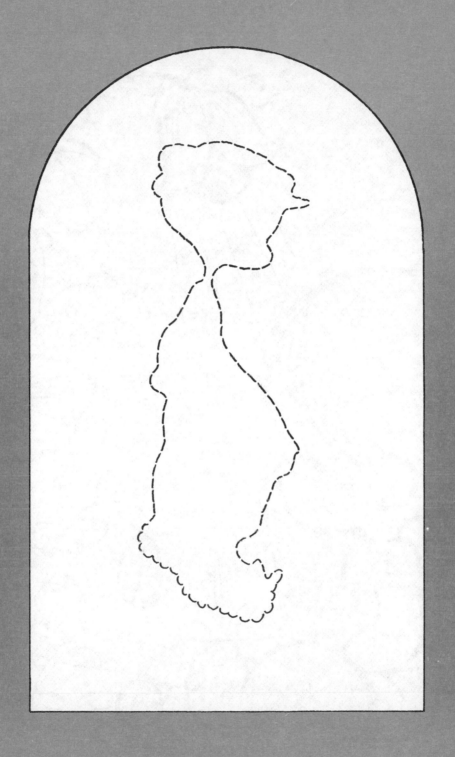

WASH YOUR TOE.

TIE A BOW.

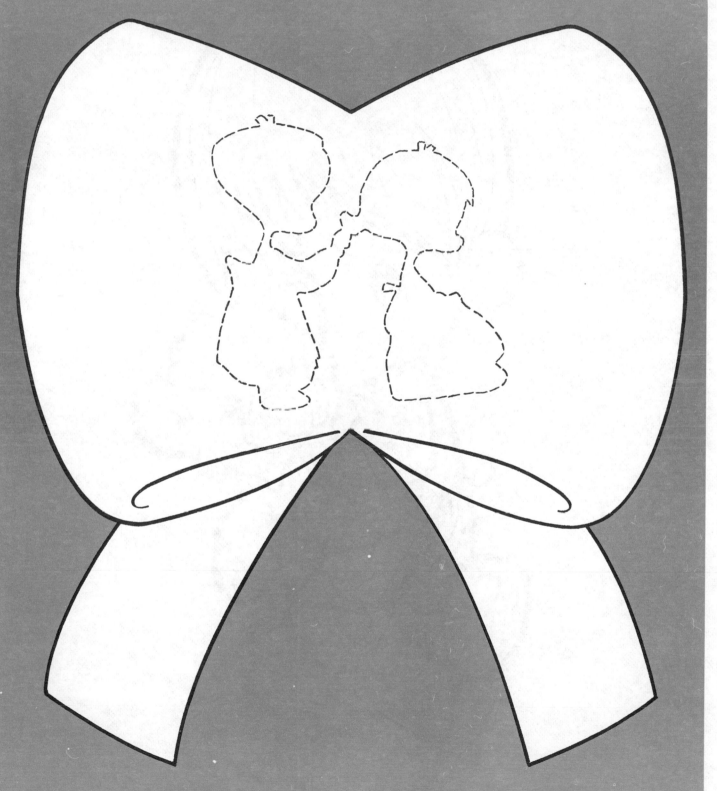

GIVE A CUDDLE.

SPLASH A PUDDLE.

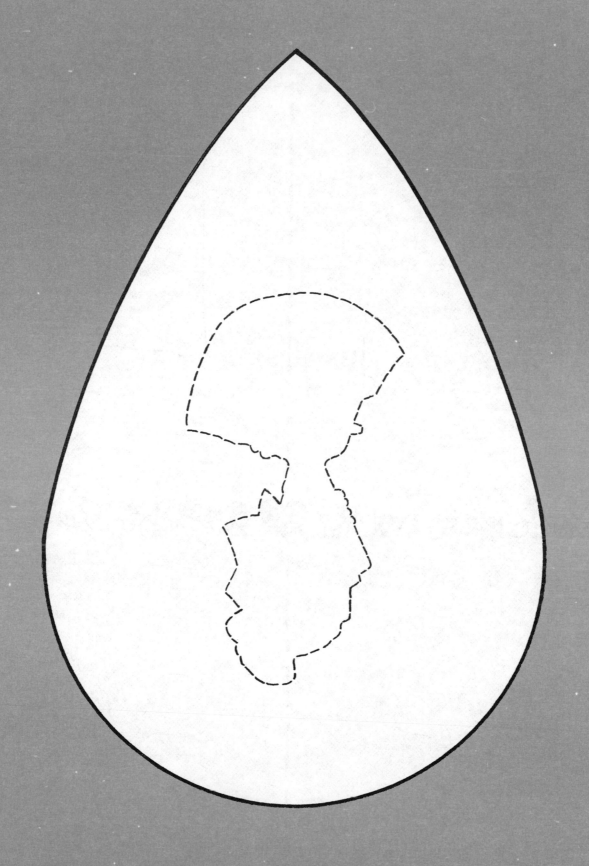

THERE ARE MANY WONDERFUL THINGS TO DO.
EVERY MOMENT IS THERE FOR YOU.

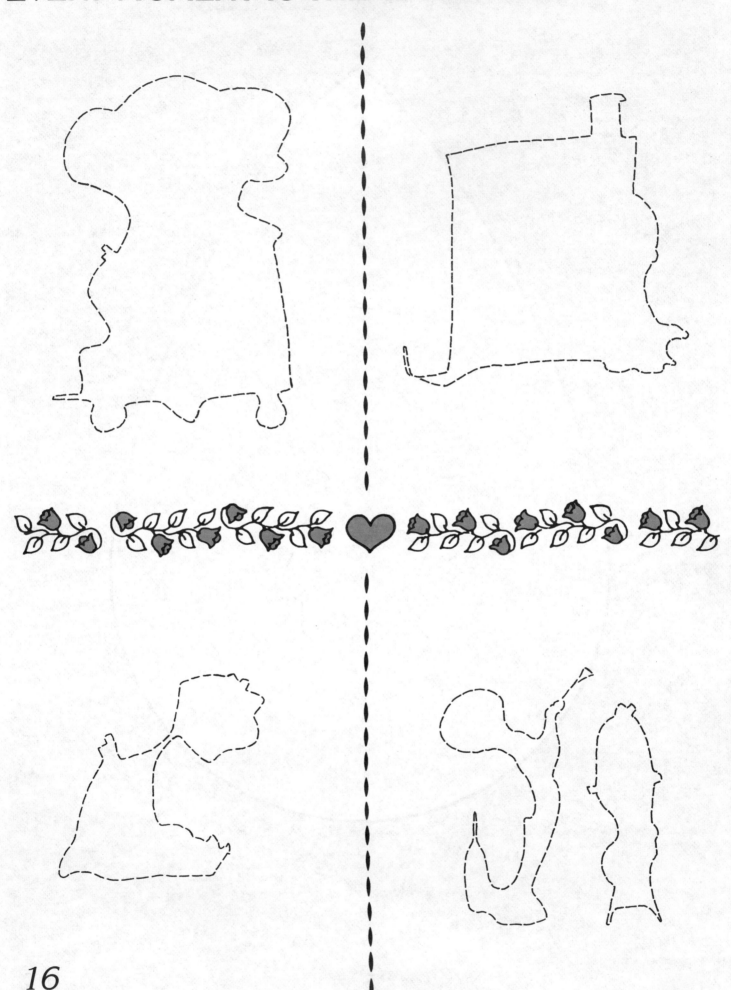